Lottie and Dottie Grow Pumpkins

There are lots of Early Reader
stories you might enjoy.

Look at the back of the book
or, for a complete list, visit
www.orionchildrensbooks.co.uk

Lottie and Dottie Grow Pumpkins

By Claire Burgess

Illustrated by
Marijke van Veldhoven

Orion
Children's Books

Orion Children's Books
First published in Great Britain in 2016 by Hodder and Stoughton

1 3 5 7 9 10 8 6 4 2

Text copyright © Claire Burgess, 2016
Illustrations copyright © Marijke van Veldhoven, 2016

The moral rights of the author and illustrator have been asserted.

A CIP catalogue record for this book
is available from the British Library.

ISBN 978 1 4440 1471 6

Printed and bound in China

The paper and board used in this book are from
well-managed forests and other responsible sources.

Orion Children's Books
An imprint of Hachette Children's Group
Part of Hodder and Stoughton
Carmelite House
50 Victoria Embankment
London EC4Y 0DZ

An Hachette UK Company

www.hachette.co.uk
www.hachettechildrens.co.uk

For my wonderful Granddad Miller,
who I helped on his allotment
many times and loved every
minute of it. – C.S.

This is Lottie and this is her little sister Dottie.

Lottie and Dottie love growing things.

This is their friend Basil from
next door. He likes growing
things too.

One day, when it was spring, Lottie and Dottie and Basil were all reading Cinderella. Dottie wondered what it would be like to be a princess.

"I love the pretty dresses," she said.
"Can we grow a pumpkin?" asked Basil.

"Of course we can," said Lottie.

They had no pumpkin seeds, so
Mum took them to the garden
centre. Mrs McWelly was there
to show them where to find
everything.

"Will the pumpkins grow really big?" asked Dottie.
"Yes, they might," said
Mrs McWelly.

When they got home they gathered

three small pots,

three labels,

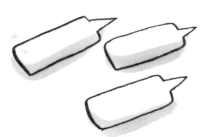

some compost

and a watering can.

Then they planted the pumpkin
seeds. There were three in the
packet so they had one each.

They filled the pots with
compost.

They patted it down gently.

Then they sowed the seeds . . .

and they watered them.

Once that was done, they labelled their pots and put them on a sunny window sill to watch them grow.

A few days later the seedlings popped through the soil.

"They're growing!" said Basil.

"They will grow much, much bigger," said Lottie.

Dottie wondered how big her
pumpkin would get.

Would it be big enough for a carriage . . .

. . . or so big she could live in it?

Soon the plants were too big for
their little pots, so they had to
put them in larger ones.

"Be careful," said Lottie as
she helped Basil and Dottie move
the plants to their new homes.

In no time at all it was time to put the pumpkin plants out in the garden.

"Where are we going to plant them?" asked Dottie.

At the end of the garden there
was a big space.
"Here will be good," said Lottie.

"They will need lots of room to
grow," said Dottie.

Basil planted his pumpkin first.
He dug a large hole.

He put his pumpkin in the
hole and then patted the earth
around it.

Dottie planted her pumpkin
next . . .

and then Lottie did hers.

"I wonder whose will be the biggest?" said Basil.
"We'll have to wait and see," said Lottie.

The days got hotter, and their
pumpkin plants grew and grew.

Dottie couldn't believe her eyes when she spotted a yellow flower.

"It won't be long until a baby pumpkin will grow from that," said Mum.

And she was right.

Mrs McWelly came to see how
their pumpkins were getting on.

She gave them a little bottle of
plant food to help the plants
grow big and strong.

"You're just like the Fairy
Godmother in Cinderella," said
Dottie.
Mrs McWelly smiled.

Basil checked on his pumpkin
every day, but one morning
he was very worried. His baby
pumpkin had started to go soft.
"What's happening?" he asked.

"Sometimes this happens," said Mum. "Don't worry, another one will grow soon."

Soon the pumpkins grew so big
that Dottie couldn't even lift
hers up.

"Wow, it's getting really big,"
said Dottie.

When the leaves began to fall off the trees and the nights got colder, it was time to harvest their pumpkins.

"This is my biggest one," said
Dottie.

"And this is mine," said Basil.

"Mine is the smallest," said Lottie.
"And a very funny shape."

"I think they all look beautiful,"
said Mum.

"What shall we do with them all?" asked Dottie.
"Let's carve one," said Mum.

Lottie, Dottie and Basil had never done that before.

Mum cut the top off, and the
children took out all the seeds.
"It's very slimy," said Dottie.

"And smelly,"
said Basil.

"Look at all the
seeds inside it,"
said Lottie.

They made a scary face. Mum put a candle inside the pumpkin and then put it outside on the front doorstep.

"What else can we do?" asked
Lottie.
"We can make soups, breads,
pies and cakes," said Mum.

"I love soup," said Dottie.

For tea that evening they had pumpkin soup and pumpkin bread, and Mum's pumpkin muffins for pudding.

Later that evening Mum, Lottie,
Dottie and Basil went out trick
or treating. They saw lots of their
friends.

Dottie was very tired when it was time for bed.

As she slept, she dreamed that she was Cinderella going to the ball.

She rode in her pumpkin pulled
by six snails and Lottie was the
footman.

How to Grow Pumpkins

Sow them in April or May.

When they get too big for their pot move them into a larger pot.

Plant them outside in June.

Water and feed as they grow.

You might see lots of bees
buzzing around the flower.

If the soil gets very wet put some
cardboard under your pumpkin
to stop it going soft.

Harvest when the leaves and
stem have gone brown.

Carve for Halloween, and make
soup, bread, pies or cakes.

What are you going to read next?

Don't miss **Lottie and Dottie** growing **carrots** and **sunflowers!**

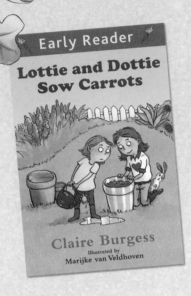

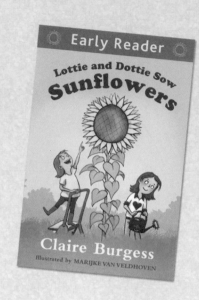

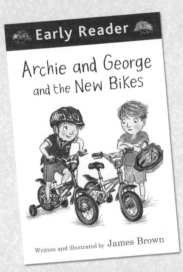

If you like **Lottie and Dottie**, you'll also enjoy **Archie and George**, who learn to ride their **own bikes,**

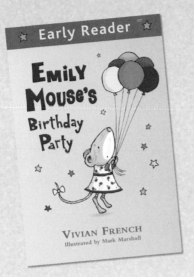

Emily Mouse's best **birthday party** ever,

and Timothy making a special mud pie in **Chocolate Porridge**.

Or visit **www.orionchildrensbooks.co.uk** to discover all the Early Readers